DATE DUE

The
SCAREBUNNY

By Dorothy Kunhardt

Illustrated by Kathy Wilburn

A GOLDEN BOOK · NEW YORK

Western Publishing Company, Inc., Racine, Wisconsin 53404

Once there was a little boy named Tam, who lived
with his mother and father in a nice house that had roses
climbing up the porch.

Tam had a little garden of his own. He grew lettuce and carrots and sweet sugar peas. Every day Tam weeded his garden. Every other day he hoed it.

One day when Tam came into his garden, he saw a
great big bunny eating a leaf of lettuce.

And the next day the bunny was there again. He had been having a feast. Oh, how he loved lettuce and carrots and peas!

The bunny even came in the rain. Tam thought, "That bad bunny won't be here today, I know." But there he was, wiggling his pink nose and chewing fast.

"Can't you see it's raining? You'll get your fur all wet,"
said Tam. "Go away. You're eating up my whole garden."
The bunny hopped away.

Tam asked his mother, "Do you have some clothes of mine that are too old and got torn by mistake?"

"Yes," said Mother. "I have some old trousers, and a shirt with quite a lot of holes, and your big straw hat that came unbraided."

"Good," said Tam. "I need a scarebunny."

Tam asked his father to build a scarebunny out of two
pieces of wood.

"If that bunny sees a scarebunny, he will think it is me,
and he will hop away," Tam said.

Tam and his mother dressed the wooden pieces in Tam's old holey clothes. On top of the make-believe head, they put the hat with its straw sticking out.

"This scarebunny will frighten him, won't it?" asked Tam.

"That's certain," said Father.

The next day when Tam went out to look at the garden, there was the bunny in a corner, eating sweet sugar peas.

And the next day he was much nearer the scarebunny, eating carrots.

And the next day he was close beside the scarebunny, eating lettuce.

Tam chased the bunny, but the bunny hopped away very slowly. He looked at Tam as if he thought Tam was a friend.

"That bad bunny isn't scared by the scarebunny, and he doesn't think it is me, and he isn't even afraid of real me any more," said Tam.

Then Tam had an idea. He divided his garden into two gardens. He drew a line down the middle with his hoe.

"Here are two nice gardens," said Tam. "I didn't need such a big garden."

Tam's father built a little picket fence around one of the half-gardens. He left the other half-garden without a fence.

The next day when the bunny saw what Tam had done for him, he hopped quickly to the garden without a fence and began to eat.

"One garden for you and one for me," said Tam.

The bunny wiggled his pink nose and chewed fast to show he was pleased.

Now every day Tam weeds, and every other day he hoes, and the bunny eats in his own garden, and they watch each other. They like to be together.

Now they really are friends.